Usborne English Readers

Level 2

Aladdin

Retold by Laura Cowan

Illustrated by Lorena Alvarez

English language consultant: Peter Viney

Contents

You can listen to the story online here:
www.usborneenglishreaders.com/
aladdin

Aladdin lived long ago in China. He was a handsome boy, but he was also very lazy. His father was dead, and he lived with his mother in the city.

Aladdin didn't like working much, so they were very poor. His mother had to make his meals and do everything for him.

One afternoon, Aladdin was walking around the market when a man stopped and spoke to him. He had a long black beard and expensive silk robes.

"Aladdin! Is it really you?" the man said. "I am your Uncle Abanazar, your father's brother. I have been in Africa for many years. I've just come back to China and heard the sad news. My dear brother is dead."

"I'm very pleased to meet you… Uncle," said Aladdin. He invited the man to his home for dinner. When he told his mother, she was surprised.

"Your father never told me about a brother," she said. "Well, we don't have much food, but I will cook something."

After their small dinner, Abanazar said, "Now that I'm home, I must take care of you, my boy. I will find you a job. Would you like that?"

"Oh," said Aladdin. He didn't want a job.

"Maybe you could work for me," said Abanazar. "You can wear expensive robes like mine, and sit in a comfortable chair all day."

Aladdin smiled. "I'm sure I can do that, Uncle."

The next morning, Abanazar bought Aladdin the most expensive robes in the city. They were made of green, blue and purple silk. Aladdin looked very important, and even more handsome than before.

"Thank you, Uncle," he said.

"I want the very best for my dear nephew," Abanazar answered. "Now, my boy, perhaps you can help me with a little job."

After his expensive present, Aladdin had to agree.

They left the city and walked for a long time, until they came to the mountains.

"Aladdin, fetch some wood and make a fire," his uncle said.

When the fire was burning, Abanazar said some words that Aladdin didn't understand. Then he took a small box from his pocket, and threw something into the fire. The sky went black. There was the sound of thunder, and a door appeared in the ground.

Aladdin wanted to run away, but Abanazar caught him. "You must be brave, nephew. Listen carefully. Below that door there is treasure, but only you can bring it out. If you do as I say, we will be the richest men in the world."

The richest men in the world? Aladdin felt braver already. "What should I do, Uncle?"

"Go through the door. Climb down, and you will find a long, narrow tunnel. There is a cave full of gold and jewels at the end. You will also see an old lamp on the ground. Take as much treasure as you want, but bring me the lamp," said Abanazar.

"A tunnel?" said Aladdin. "Is it dark? I can't do it, Uncle! I'm afraid of the dark."

Abanazar took off one of his rings. "If you are frightened, this ring will help you," he said. "Now go."

Aladdin climbed through the door and into the tunnel below. He walked until he came to a beautiful garden full of golden trees. Instead of fruit, the trees grew bright red, blue and green jewels. Near one of the trees, Aladdin found a dusty lamp.

"Why does he want this old thing?" Aladdin wondered. He put it in his robe, then filled his pockets with jewels.

Aladdin went back through the tunnel,
but the treasure was heavy in his pockets.
He couldn't climb up to the door.

"Help me, Uncle," Aladdin said.

"Give me the lamp first."

"I can't, Uncle. My hands are full."

Abanazar was angry. "Stupid boy! I'm
not your uncle. I am the wizard Abanazar,
and you can't trick me. Do you really want
the lamp? You can stay down there with it
forever." He closed the door and disappeared.

Uncle! Please don't leave me!" Aladdin called, but there was no answer. He was alone in the dark.

He rubbed his cold hands together. His fingers rubbed Abanazar's ring.

Suddenly there was a puff of smoke, and a big green genie appeared.

"I am the genie of the ring. What do you want from me?" he asked.

Aladdin was very frightened, but he said, "Can you take me back to the city?"

"Your wish is my command, master," the genie answered, and immediately Aladdin was at home again.

"Thank you," said Aladdin, but the genie wasn't there. Aladdin found his mother and told her all about Abanazar. She took the jewels and the lamp.

"Oh, these are beautiful. We can sell them at the market," she said, "Maybe we can sell this old lamp, too. It's very dirty, but I can clean it."

She started to rub the lamp, and there was another puff of smoke.

A blue genie appeared. He was twice as big as the first genie. "I am the genie of the lamp," he said. "What do you want from me?"

"We're very hungry," said Aladdin. "Can you bring us some food?"

"Your wish is my command," said the genie, and he brought golden plates full of delicious meat and bread, cakes and fruit.

The next day, Aladdin sold the plates at the market for lots of money. After that, Aladdin and his mother lived very well. The genie brought them food every night, and in the morning Aladdin sold the golden plates.

A few months later, Aladdin looked out one day and saw the Emperor's soldiers in the streets. "The Emperor's daughter, Princess Moon Flower, wishes to visit the city baths. Everyone must stay at home. No one must look at her!" they shouted.

Aladdin wanted to see this famous princess. He quickly went to the baths, hid nearby and waited.

When the Princess arrived, Aladdin couldn't believe his eyes. There were many beautiful women in the city, but Princess Moon Flower was a thousand times more beautiful.

That night he told his mother, "I think I'm in love with the Princess. I must talk to her."

"Oh, Aladdin," said his mother, "I don't think that's going to happen."

"The genies will help me," said Aladdin. He fetched the lamp and rubbed it. Immediately the blue genie appeared.

"Bring the Princess Moon Flower here to me," Aladdin said.

"Your wish is my command," said the genie, and he brought the Princess to Aladdin's house. When Aladdin's mother saw Moon Flower, she fell on her knees.

"Where am I?" asked the Princess. "Who are you?"

Aladdin stepped forward, "Don't be frightened, Princess. I just wanted to meet you. Please, sit down."

So Moon Flower sat down and they talked. In the morning, the genie took her back to the Emperor's palace. Every night for a week, the genie brought Moon Flower to Aladdin's house, and every morning he took her home again. Soon she was waiting for the evenings so that she could be with Aladdin.

Aladdin said to his mother, "Take these jewels to the Emperor. Tell him that your son wants to marry the Princess."

Aladdin's mother went to the Emperor's enormous palace with a golden plate full of jewels. She waited and waited, but the Emperor was very busy. She went back every day until the Emperor spoke to her.

"So your son wants to marry my daughter," the Emperor said, looking at the jewels. They were bigger and more beautiful than anything in his treasure room.

"She needs a husband, it's true. Your son can marry her – if he brings me forty more bowls full of jewels like these."

Of course the genie soon brought the jewels, and the next day Aladdin arrived at the palace in his best silk robes. Forty men in blue robes followed him. They were carrying the golden bowls. When the Emperor saw them, he agreed to the marriage immediately.

Aladdin asked the genie to build a home for him and Moon Flower. In only one night, the genie built a wonderful palace opposite the Emperor's. It had a hundred rooms and a thousand windows. All around were beautiful gardens full of flowers, birds and tall trees.

Aladdin married the Princess the next day. They rode through the city on two white horses, and Aladdin threw money to the people. Everyone cheered and cheered. Everyone was happy.

Everyone was happy, except for one man. Far away in the mountains, Abanazar heard about the marriage. "So Aladdin stole my lamp, and now he has a new wife and a beautiful palace? Well, there's going to be trouble."

Abanazar went back to the city. This time
he dressed in old clothes, not in his silk
robes. One morning, he waited for Aladdin
to leave his palace, then he stood in the
street and shouted "New lamps for old!
Bring me your old lamps and I will give you
new ones!"

The Princess heard him. "Aladdin has a
dusty old lamp," she said. "I'll get him a
nice new one instead." She ran outside with
the magic lamp.

Abanazar laughed and rubbed the lamp
in his hands. The enormous blue genie
appeared with a puff of smoke.

"Carry the Princess to Africa with me, and
bring Aladdin's palace too," Abanazar said.

"Your wish is my command, master."

Later that day, the Emperor looked out
of his window. "Where's Aladdin's palace?
Where's my daughter?" he shouted. "Aladdin
has tricked me! Bring him to me now."

Aladdin fell on his knees. "I haven't done anything wrong. I love the Princess, and you are like a father to me. I don't know what's happened, but I will bring Moon Flower back, and the palace too."

Aladdin put on his ring. The big green genie appeared.

"Bring back the Princess and my palace," Aladdin commanded.

"I can't do that, master" the genie said sadly, "This is the work of the genie of the lamp. He is much stronger than I am, and I can't change his magic – but I can take you to the palace instead."

Soon Aladdin was outside his palace again. He waited in the gardens until the Princess came out. "Moon Flower," Aladdin called quietly, "Moon Flower."

The Princess looked around and saw her husband. "Oh, Aladdin! I'm so happy to see you. Abanazar says that he's going to kill you, and then he wants to marry me!"

"Don't worry. I have a plan," Aladdin said. He gave her a little silver bottle. "Put some drops from this bottle in his dinner when he's not looking. After he eats it, he will go to sleep. Be brave. I'll watch through the window."

The Princess went into the palace. Abanazar was sitting at the table with two golden plates full of food. "Are you hungry, my dear?"

"No, Abanazar. Perhaps you would like to eat mine, too?" said Moon Flower. She picked up her plate. When Abanazar wasn't looking, she put a few drops from the little bottle on to the food. The wizard ate everything, and soon he was asleep at the table.

Aladdin ran into the palace. He quickly found the lamp and rubbed it. The big blue genie appeared.

"Take Abanazar far away, so far away that he can never come back," said Aladdin. "Then carry me and the Princess and our palace back home."

The genie picked up the sleeping wizard, and left him on a tiny island in the middle of the sea.

Then he brought the palace back to the city with Aladdin and Moon Flower inside. When the Emperor saw them again, he was so happy that he cried.

After that, Aladdin and Moon Flower lived happily. They had lots of children, and in time Aladdin became Emperor. The wizard Abanazar never left his island, and the lamp and the ring stayed in the palace treasure room. Perhaps they are still there. Who knows? Maybe the genies are still inside.

About the story

The story of Aladdin comes from a collection of stories called *One Thousand and One Nights*. The collection is over a thousand years old, and different people added stories to it over many years. There are hundreds of magical stories from all over Asia, North Africa and the Middle East.

The first story is about a young woman called Shahrazad. Her husband, the king, plans to kill her, so she starts telling him a story. She doesn't finish it, so the king lets her live for another day, and then another... She tells story after story for a thousand and one nights, until the king realizes that he loves her.

You might know a few other stories from the *Thousand and One Nights*. Two of the most famous are *Ali Baba* and *Sinbad the Sailor*. Today you can see plays, movies and musicals about Aladdin all around the world.

Activities

The answers are on page 40.

Your wish is my command

Choose a word to finish each sentence.

1.

"Can you.......us some food?"

bring   carry   make

2.

"...... Aladdin's palace to Africa."

Fly   Send   Carry

3.

"I can't ....that, master."

say   help   do

4.

"........ Abanazar far away."

Bring   Take   Put

Mixed-up story

Can you put these pictures and sentences in order?

A.

Aladdin married the Princess the next day.

B.

"Don't worry. I have a plan," Aladdin said.

C.

A blue genie appeared. He was twice as big as the first genie.

D.

They had lots of children, and in time, Aladdin became Emperor.

E.

Abanazar stood in the street and shouted, "New lamps for old!"

F.

"There is a cave full of gold and jewels at the end."

G.

"I am your Uncle Abanazar, your father's brother."

H.

When the Princess arrived, Aladdin couldn't believe his eyes.

I.

"I am the genie of the ring. What do you want from me?"

The people in the story

Choose *two* sentences for each person.

Aladdin   Abanazar   Princess   Aladdin's
                         Moon Flower   mother

A.
She has to do
everything for Aladdin.

B.
She's the most beautiful
woman in the city.

C.
He says he's
Aladdin's uncle.

D.
He doesn't like
working.

E.
She gives Abanazar
the magic lamp.

F.
He tricks Princess
Moon Flower.

G.
He falls in love with
Princess Moon Flower.

H.
She goes to the
palace every day.

City streets

Which three things *can't* you see?

Aladdin   Princess   soldiers
               Moon Flower

a plate of food   a tree   a palace

a baby   a magic lamp

Abanazar says...

Choose the right ending for each sentence.

"I've just come back to China and...

A ...bought these silk robes."
B ...heard the sad news."

"If you do as I say...

A ...you will be the bravest man in the world."
B ...we will be the richest men in the world."

"Take as much treasure as you want, but...

A ...bring me the lamp."
B ...don't take the ring."

"Bring me your old lamps and...

A ...I will take them away!"
B ...I will give you new ones!"

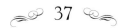

Word list

appear (v) when something appears,
it is suddenly there or you can see it.

baths (n pl) before people had bathrooms in their
houses, they used to go to public baths to wash.

beard (n) hair that grows around
and below a man's mouth.

cheer (v) when you cheer, you shout
to show that you're happy.

command (n) an instruction that you have to follow.

drop (n) a tiny amount of water or other liquid.

dusty (adj) if something is dusty, it is
covered in a thin layer of dirt because it
hasn't been moved or used for a long time.

emperor (n) an emperor is like a king,
but even more powerful and important.

forever (adv) for the rest of time.

genie (n) a powerful magical creature.

immediately (adv) very quickly,
almost at the same time.

knee (n) the part that bends in the middle of your leg.

lamp (n) something that gives you
light, especially in your home.

marriage (n) a marriage is when two people get married.

master (n) you call someone 'master' if you are their servant.

nephew (n) your nephew is your brother's son or your sister's son.

puff of smoke (n) a small amount of smoke that appears suddenly.

robes (n pl) something that you wear. They are usually long and loose.

rub (v) when you move your hand quickly backwards and forwards over something, you rub it.

silk (n) a soft, expensive material that is nice to wear.

step (v) when you put one foot forward, you take a step.

thunder (n) the loud noise that you hear during a storm. You hear it after you see lightning.

tiny (adj) very, very small.

treasure (n) lots of valuable and expensive things together, like gold and silver and jewels.

tunnel (n) a way under the ground or through rock.

uncle (n) your uncle is your father's brother or your mother's brother.

Answers

Your wish is my command

1. bring
2. carry
3. do
4. take

Mixed-up story

G, F, I, C, H,
A, E, B, D

The people in the story

Aladdin – D, G
Abanazar – C, F
Princess Moon Flower – B, E
Aladdin's mother – A, H

City streets

Princess Moon Flower
a magic lamp
a palace

Abanazar says...

1. B
2. B
3. A
4. B

You can find information about other
Usborne English Readers here:
www.usborneenglishreaders.com

Designed by Laura Nelson Norris
Edited by Mairi Mackinnon
Digital imaging: Nick Wakeford and John Russell
With thanks to Ian McNee

First published in 2017 by Usborne Publishing Ltd.,
Usborne House, 83-85 Saffron Hill, London EC1N 8RT, England.
www.usborne.com Copyright © 2017 Usborne Publishing Ltd.